Animals
Butterflies

by Nick Rebman

FOCUS
READERS

www.focusreaders.com

Focus Readers is distributed by North Star Editions:
sales@northstareditions.com | 888-417-0195

Produced for Focus Readers by Red Line Editorial.

Photographs ©: Sean Xu/Shutterstock Images, cover, 1; Jag_cz/Shutterstock Images, 4; Ambient Ideas/Shutterstock Images, 4; Cbenjasuwan/Shutterstock Images, 7, 16 (top left); Mathisa/Shutterstock Images, 9, 16 (bottom left), 16 (bottom right); Roberto Michel/Shutterstock Images, 11; anekoho/Shutterstock Images, 13; Kate Besler/Shutterstock Images, 15; Olga Danylenko/Shutterstock Images, 16 (top right)

ISBN
978-1-63517-845-6 (hardcover)
978-1-63517-946-0 (paperback)
978-1-64185-149-7 (ebook pdf)
978-1-64185-048-3 (hosted ebook)

Library of Congress Control Number: 2018931092

Printed in the United States of America
Mankato, MN
May, 2018

About the Author

Nick Rebman enjoys reading, drawing, and traveling to places where he doesn't speak the language. He lives in Minnesota.

Table of Contents

Butterflies

Butterflies are colorful.

Some are red.

Some are blue.

Some are yellow.

A butterfly has

two **antennae**.

A butterfly has four wings.

A butterfly has six legs.

antennae

wing

leg

Behavior

A butterfly starts life as

a **caterpillar**.

It forms a **shell**.

It changes inside the shell.

It becomes a butterfly.

caterpillar

shell

butterfly

9

Butterflies live all over
the world.
Some live in fields.
Some live in **forests**.

forest

Food

Most butterflies eat nectar.

Nectar comes from flowers.

Nectar is sweet.

Butterflies do not live long.

Some live for a week.

Some live for a month.

Some live for a year.

Glossary

antennae

forests

caterpillar

shell

Index

C
color, 5

N
nectar, 12

S
shell, 8

W
wings, 6